BOOK ANALYSIS

By Cassandra Gibbons

Normal People

BY SALLY ROONEY

BrightSummaries.com

SALLY ROONEY

IRISH NOVELIST

- **Born in Castlebar in 1991.**
- **Notable works:**
  - *Mr Salary* (2016), short story
  - *Conversations with Friends* (2017), novel
  - *Normal People* (2018), novel

Sally Rooney is an Irish novelist who was born in Castlebar, County Mayo in 1991. She grew up with two siblings and moved to Dublin to study English at Trinity College, where she was elected a scholar and participated in debating; she went on to participate in the European University Debating Championships in 2013. After her undergraduate degree in English, she completed a Masters in American Literature. She currently lives in Dublin.

Rooney wrote her first novel, *Conversations with Friends*, while completing her Masters degree. After an auction for the publication rights, this debut novel was published in 2017 and nominated for a slew of prizes. The novel was well received by critics and Rooney herself was hailed as a remarkable addition to the modern Irish canon, being dubbed the "Salinger for the Snapchat generation" by her editor at Faber & Faber. In the same year her short story *Mr Salary* was nominated for the Sunday Times EFG Private Bank Short Story Award.

NORMAL PEOPLE

A DUAL-PERSPECTIVE NOVEL

- **Genre:** modern fiction
- **Reference edition:** Rooney, S. (2018) *Normal People*. London: Faber & Faber.
- **1st edition:** 2018
- **Themes:** class, relationships, Irish society, domestic violence, university education

Normal People tells the story of Connell and Marianne, two students (who move from high school to university over the course of the novel) who have an on-off romantic relationship. The novel was the highly anticipated follow-up to Rooney's critically adored debut *Conversations with Friends*. *Normal People* cemented Rooney's status as a first-class writer, and attracted accolades including 'Irish Novel of the Year' at the Irish Book Awards and 'Best Novel of the Year' at the Costa Book Awards. The novel was also named the 'Waterstones Book of the Year' and was longlisted for the 2018 Man Booker Prize.

Normal People is written in the third person, and alternates between the perspectives of the two characters. The chapters are dated and distributed sporadically over the characters' student timeline, with gaps in between that generally range between a few weeks and a few months in duration (although a few are much shorter). The novel alternates between the use of the present tense (when describing the events of the eponymous chapter date) and the past tense, in which the reader is caught up with the events of periods that fall between the dated chapters.

SUMMARY

HIGH SCHOOL

Marianne and Connell attend the same high school in Carricklea, but they do not interact at school. The only time they talk is when Connell picks up his mother, Lorraine, from Marianne's house, where Lorraine works as a cleaner. Marianne is a loner in high school, and considered by most to be weird and unsociable. This is in stark contrast to Connell, who is popular, though quiet, and a star of the school football team. Nevertheless, he finds himself drawn to Marianne, and their conversations about their economics teacher (who flirts inappropriately with Connell) and literature lead to a kiss and the start of a secret relationship.

Connell stipulates that the relationship must remain a secret because he fears the damage a relationship with Marianne would do to his reputation. Marianne agrees and promises not to tell anyone but begins to resent the arrangement. She brings up his friends' bullying behaviour towards her, and although Connell feels guilty, he does nothing to defend her and continues to hide the relationship. Despite the fear of being found out, Connell is comfortable in his relationship with Marianne. He feels comfortable having sex with her because he knows she will not tell anyone about their shared intimacy, something that previous girlfriends have aired publicly. Marianne is applying to study History and Politics at Trinity College, Dublin, and encourages Connell to apply for English there, which he does.

Marianne is thrust into Connell's social circle when she is voted onto the fundraising committee for the Debs (a school dance). Both she and Connell attend a fundraising event where Marianne is treated kindly by some of his friends, like Karen, and less so by others, like Rachel (who wants to be Connell's girlfriend). Marianne is groped by Pat, who attended the high school at the same time as Marianne's brother, Alan, and is laughed at by some of Connell's friends, including Rachel. Connell plucks up the courage to ask Rachel "would you ever fuck off?" (p. 41) and drives Marianne home. Marianne stays overnight at Connell's house and he tells her he loves her for the first time.

Despite Connell's feelings for Marianne, he asks Rachel to the Debs out of concern for his reputation and the anxiety that his double life is inflicting on him. Marianne drops out of school and studies for her exams independently at home. Connell and Rachel are incompatible and their relationship is short-lived. Despite their respective heartaches, both Connell and Marianne do well in their final exams and prepare to move to the capital for university. Eric, one of Connell's friends, tells Connell that everyone was aware of his relationship with Marianne and that nobody cared. Connell is devastated to realise that he has thrown away his relationship with Marianne for nothing.

> "Do you think we don't know you were riding her? he [Eric] said. Sure everyone knows. ... This was probably the most horrifying thing Eric could have said to him [Connell], not because it ended his life, but because it didn't. He knew then that the secret for which he had sacrificed his own happiness and the happiness of another person had been trivial all along, and worthless." (p. 77)

UNIVERSITY

Connell and Marianne bump into each other at a student party in Dublin to find that they have switched places on the social ladder. Marianne is popular, has a boyfriend and is considered cool and attractive by a lot of people. Connell, on the other hand, is largely friendless and struggling to fit in. Six months into their degrees, despite both of them having had flings with other people, Marianne forgives Connell for shunning her at school and the two restart their sexual relationship. They continue to avoid defining their relationship, although it is patently obvious to their friends that they are romantically involved.

A miscommunication pushes Marianne and Connell apart for a second time. Connell is unable to afford rent in Dublin for the summer holidays, and tells Marianne in the hope that she will let him stay with her (she lives alone in a flat belonging to a family member). Marianne misunderstands his meaning, and assumes that he is telling her he is going home. Unable to steer the conversation back towards a solution in which they can spend the summer together,

Connell miserably suggests that they see other people. Asking to stay with her rent-free feels too much like asking for money to him, and money is something that the pair has never openly discussed.

Marianne ignores Connell's messages over the next few months, but bumps into him in Carricklea over the summer. They tentatively get back on speaking terms and Connell attends Marianne's father's memorial mass to support her. Marianne is now seeing someone from a wealthy background called Jamie, and Connell deals with his resentment by imagining that Marianne wanted to break up with him in order to find a richer boyfriend, even though he knows it is not true. Connell drunkenly goes home with his old economics teacher, who used to flirt with him, and is almost pressured into sex, but manages to get home unscathed.

Marianne and Connell meet for coffee in Dublin during their second year. Marianne tells Connell that Jamie likes to beat her up during sex, but that she has to fake willing submission with him – she never had to fake wanting to submit to Connell's will. Meanwhile, Connell has started seeing someone else, a medical student named Helen, and has fallen in love with her. Marianne cries when Connell tells her this Connell finally admits that he was hoping to stay at Marianne's apartment the previous summer, and they realise that they have once again broken up for no good reason.

EUROPE AND BEYOND

Both Connell and Marianne pass the scholarship exams, which entitle them to free university accommodation, free tuition (up to Masters level) and a free meal every night in college. Connell is able to go travelling around Europe with friends thanks to his newfound financial security. He is deeply in love with Helen, or at least with the idea of having a normal girlfriend, but still constantly emails Marianne to discuss politics, literature and their past. Helen and Marianne both make an effort to get on well for Connell's sake, but Helen finds Marianne to be self-absorbed and promiscuous and Connell struggles to defend Marianne. Connell and his friends meet up with Marianne, Jamie and Marianne's friend Peggy in Trieste, where a dinner party descends into a row between Marianne and her boyfriend. Connell and Marianne share a bed that night and kiss, but do not have sex because of Helen.

Marianne breaks up with Jamie and goes to Sweden for her third year on an Erasmus exchange. She and Connell continue to email each other constantly. Marianne's Swedish boyfriend, Lukas, degrades her sexually just like Jamie did, and even takes photos of her naked body. Marianne eventually leaves him, and returns to Carricklea for Connell's friend Rob's funeral. Connell takes Helen to the funeral but shares a lingering hug with Marianne in the church: Helen and Connell break up soon after. Connell falls into a deep depression following Rob's death (from suicide) and goes to the university counselling service. He becomes more involved in the literary society in Marianne's absence, and even consents to having a short story published in the university literary magazine, albeit under a pseudonym.

The summer following Marianne's return from Norway, Connell and Marianne reconnect in Carricklea, where Marianne is spending all her time and Connell is spending weekends.

Although they stop short of reinitiating their sexual relationship, they spend most of their time together. After a night out, they discuss their romantic relationship and decide to try again. Their reunion sex ends awkwardly when Marianne asks Connell to hit her, which he does not want to do. Marianne goes home, where she is tormented by her abusive brother, Alan. He tries to get into her room by kicking the door in. Marianne is hit hard in the face by the door (she was standing on the other side trying to keep it closed) and bleeds profusely. She calls Connell, who takes her back to his house, but not before threatening to kill Alan if he ever hurts Marianne again. Connell tells Marianne he loves her in the car.

Following Alan's assault of Marianne, she stops seeing her family. She spends the following Christmas with Connell and Lorraine and is ignored by her mother when they cross paths in the supermarket. After Christmas Connell is accepted onto a Masters programme in Creative Writing at a university in New York. Marianne is surprised he did not tell her about his application, and a little hurt that he did tell Sadie, with whom he works on the literary magazine. Connell is unsure about accepting, and tells Marianne that if she wants him to stay in Ireland, he will. Marianne suspects that Connell may stay in America after the Masters, or that he might come back changed and their relationship will no longer be viable. Nonetheless, she encourages him to go and reassures him that she will always be there for him.

CHARACTER STUDY

MARIANNE

Marianne is an intelligent young woman who speaks bluntly and with little consideration for social mores. She is introduced to the reader as an outsider in her high school, where she has no friends and spends her free time reading novels and deflecting bullying comments. She is drawn to the popular Connell, though she knows better than to approach him at school. She strikes up a secret relationship with him outside of school hours, and although Connell returns her feelings, he is unable to commit to a public relationship with her because he fears he will suffer reputational damage from being associated with her odd behaviour.

> "Marianne had a row with her History teacher, Mr Kerrigan, last year because he caught her looking out a window during class... it seemed so obviously insane to her then that... even her eye movements fell under the jurisdiction of school rules. You're not learning if you're staring out the

> window, Mr Kerrigan said. Marianne, who had lost her temper by then, snapped back: Don't delude yourself, I have nothing to learn from you." (p. 13)

Marianne's father died when she was younger, and she has bad relationships with her mother, Denise, and her brother, Alan. Alan physically abuses her, as did her father. Denise has always failed to defend her daughter against both men, and tells her daughter that she, Marianne, is cold and unlovable. Marianne clearly takes this to heart, and thinks that she is unpopular because of her cold personality. She seeks to be a sexual submissive in her relationships with men, and finds some men, like Jamie and Lukas, who are willing to degrade her. Her relationship with Connell is different because she truly wants to submit to him, and finds that she is able to achieve this without him hitting her.

Marianne experiences an upsurge of popularity at university due to her conversational skills and academic brilliance, but falls from grace after her ex-boyfriend, Jamie, spreads gossip about her throughout the campus. Few of her friends stand by her, and her friend Peggy actively shuns her. She reflects that her unconventional personality has always been a problem for men, who have tried to bring her down because of it, with the exception of Connell. Marianne, unlike Connell, is able to deal with her unpopularity with a cool detachment.

> "...everyone has to pretend not to notice that their social lives are arranged hierarchically, with certain people at the top... and others lower down. Marianne sometimes sees herself at the very bottom of the ladder, but at other times she pictures herself off the ladder completely, not affected by its mechanics, since she does not actually desire popularity or do anything to make it belong to her." (p. 29)

CONNELL

Connell is a popular student with a keen academic mind and love of literature who lives with his single mother, Lorraine, and does not know the identity of his father. His sporting prowess, good grades and popularity at school defy the low expectations that so often face working class children of single parents. He is determined to succeed despite his lack of financial means, even considering studying a subject that does not interest him (Law) because it could result in a lucrative career. Connell considers his popularity and normality to be a part of his success, and his wish to maintain them drives him to misery and anxiety.

Connell is drawn to Marianne despite the consensus amongst his peers that she is weird and ugly. He feels completely relaxed around her sexually because he trusts her to keep their private life private, although he suffers from severe social anxiety due to his attraction to a girl who is socially considered to be unattractive. He periodically ends his relationship with her for the wrong reasons: a misguided attempt to maintain his reputation, a miscommunication between them and a desire to have a 'normal' girlfriend. Despite these hiccups in their relationship, Marianne and Connell are drawn to each other again and again, and never fail to look out for one another.

Connell struggles to fit in at university because of the class difference between him and his peers. As his university career goes on and he finds financial stability thanks to his scholarship, he is able to involve himself more in university life. This involves taking on a role at the student literary magazine, first as a contributing writer (under a pseudonym) and then as editor. He suffers a severe depressive episode after the suicide of one of his school friends, Rob, which he combats using medication. By the end of the novel he is confident enough to apply for a Masters in Creative Writing at a university in New York, but offers to put Marianne first by turning it down and staying with her in their renewed relationship. The novel ends as she encourages him to take the opportunity.

LORRAINE

Lorraine is Connell's mother and works as a cleaner, initially at Marianne's house. Lorraine is kind, loving and proud of her son, though not to the extent that she will overlook his bad behaviour. When she finds out that Connell is taking Rachel to the Debs instead of Marianne, Lorraine tells him in no uncertain terms that she is disgusted with him and comforts Marianne. Nonetheless, after this outburst she continues to support her son in his decisions, and reassures him that she has no regrets in having him, even if becoming a teenage single mother might not have been the best thing for her. Lorraine is perhaps the best example in the novel of the idea that people who enjoy a better standard of living are not necessarily better people.

ALAN

Alan is Marianne's older brother who abuses her both physically and psychologically. Aided by their mother, Denise, Alan destroys Marianne's sense of her self by constantly telling her how unlovable and unworthy she is. He undermines her confidence at every opportunity and is enraged by her calm, detached attempts to shake him off. This often leads to violence, and culminates in Alan injuring (and possibly breaking) Marianne's nose by slamming a door into her face in an attempt to get into her bedroom. Alan is defined by his cowardice: he calls for his mother when Connell threatens him after the door incident, and cries when Connell warns him to never hurt Marianne again.

HELEN

Helen is a medical student who dates Connell when he is in the middle of his degree. She is kind, loving, and above all, a normal person, in Connell's eyes. He considers himself to be deeply in love with her, but continues to communicate with Marianne by email throughout his relationship with Helen. He is put off by some of Helen's old-fashioned views (she thinks Marianne is "slutty" [p. 168], for example) and is uncomfortable with her overall dislike of Marianne. Despite the bliss of normality Connell experiences when he is with Helen, their relationship flounders in the wake of Rob's suicide and the beginnings of Connell's depression.

ANALYSIS

CLASS

Social class is an omnipresent theme throughout the novel, which includes characters of different backgrounds and different financial positions. Marianne is born into a wealthy family and lives in a large house, whereas Connell is born to a teenage single mother who works as a cleaner. While this disparity does nothing to alter the pair's feelings for each other, money becomes a delicate issue for them to navigate in their relationship. The two often avoid talking about their respective social classes. Marianne is self-conscious about her wealth, and when discussing class and money with Connell she adopts a more sensitive tone, eschewing her normal bluntness, in order to avoid making him feel uncomfortable.

> "I guess we're from very different backgrounds, class-wise. [said Connell.] I don't think about it much, she said. Quickly she added: Sorry, that's an ignorant thing to say. Maybe I should think about it more." (p. 173)

Connell justifies his decision to end the relationship on two occasions by convincing himself that his relationship with Marianne cannot overcome the class divide, even though he knows that she is not materialistic. Lorraine mentions to him in conversation that Marianne's mother Denise might not like Connell as a potential boyfriend for her daughter because of the class difference between the two. Connell latches onto this argument as a reason why the relationship is doomed because he cannot bring himself to either have a public relationship with Marianne and risk his reputation, or end it because of her lack of popularity. When Connell regrets breaking up with Marianne at university because he felt uncomfortable asking her if he could stay at her apartment over summer, he convinces himself that she was hoping to rid herself of him in order to find a richer boyfriend.

While Marianne's boyfriend Jamie is much richer than Connell, he proves to be cruel, uncaring and vengeful, spreading malicious gossip about Marianne after their breakup. Marianne has a much more successful cross-class relationship with Connell that she does with any of her wealthier peers. The novel strongly promotes social integration, as well as the idea that money does not buy happiness, nor is it a guarantor of a good personality. The characterisation of Lorraine and Marianne's mother Denise is perhaps the starkest contrast between the classes in the novel. Lorraine is kind-hearted, to the extent that she worries about Marianne as well as her own child. Middle-class Denise, on the other hand, is cold and cruel to her daughter, tearing down her self-esteem at any given opportunity. Marianne is also shunned by her middle-class friends at university (with the exception of Joanna) after her break-up with Jamie. The overarching message of the novel is that a higher social class is no indicator of good character. It could even be argued that Rooney deliberately presents middle-class characters in a negative light. Marianne is the exception to the rule in a novel that portrays most of the wealthier characters as superficial (such as Marianne's friend Peggy) or even downright abusive (for example, Alan).

NORMALITY

Both Marianne and Connell are preoccupied with being – or even just being seen as – normal. They both long for a life free of complications, even if other people's ideas of normality are not right for them. This is perhaps most obvious in Connell's relationship with Helen, which he considers to be the pinnacle of normal relationships. His love for her is confused by the fact that he is happy to have achieved a sense of normality, and he ignores his doubts about her because he is loath to give up his conventional relationship. He finds himself cutting conversations with her short because he wants to savour the aftermath rather than actually speak to her, he is put off by her somewhat conservative views and, most importantly, he cannot stop himself from composing long emails to Marianne while he is in a relationship with Helen. The relationship is wrong for Connell but he convinces himself that it is right because the illusion of normality feels right. His self-description of 'acceptable' in the below quotation conveys that he thought of himself as an unacceptable person when he was with Marianne, which shows how deep his obsession with public image runs.

> "To be known as her boyfriend plants him firmly in the social world, establishes him as an acceptable person, someone with a particular status, someone whose conversational silences are thoughtful rather than socially awkward." (p. 155)

Marianne's attitude to normality is different to Connell's but by no means less profound. Having been told repeatedly by the mother and brother while growing up (and most likely by her father too – it is implied that he was also abusive) that she is abnormal, Marianne has processed and seemingly accepted this fact. She is blunt in high school even when it destroys her popularity. She retains her originality in her relationship with Connell, but stops short of telling him that her family are abusive. She later admits to him that she thought he would not want her if she was damaged. By the end of the novel, Marianne feels that after going from being hated in high school to the heights of popularity at university, she has finally reached equilibrium. Connell seems to have achieved a similar level of contentedness in his relationship with Marianne. The novel seems to conclude that their acceptance of themselves and each other has brought them the normality that they so craved, even though certain things, such as Marianne's abusive upbringing and Connell's depression, still fall outside of the norm. They are normal people nonetheless: "Marianne is neither admired nor reviled anymore. People have forgotten about her. She's a normal person now." (p. 254)

STRUCTURE AND PERSPECTIVE

Normal People does not adhere to a strict chronology. The chapter titles all follow a chronological pattern and are called 'Seven Months Later', 'Six Weeks Later' and so on. The month and the year are given underneath the chapter titles so that the reader can easily date events. Much of the novel is written in the present tense and details events that happen in the eponymous time period of each chapter. Certain sections, however, are written in the past tense and detail events that happened in the time periods in between chapters. These segments could be described as flashbacks, and serve the purpose of clarifying earlier events and revealing the characters' motives. One example of this retrospective clarifying of events is Marianne and Connell's second break-up, after their months together at university. The supermarket scene, in which Marianne bumps into Connell and Lorraine, is when the reader first learns that the couple have stopped seeing each other romantically. This is narrated from Marianne's perspective (though still in the third person): "He said he wanted to see other people and she said: Okay" (p. 110).

This comes as a shock given that, in the previous chapter, Marianne and Connell were getting on well. It is only in the following chapter, more of which is told from Connell's perspective, that we see the break-up scene being played out in flashback. It becomes apparent that Connell did not want to break up with Marianne, that she misinterpreted his words about moving home for the summer and he failed to correct her due to a crippling anxiety about money. This miscommunication is mirrored with a smaller misunderstanding towards the end of the novel. Marianne asks Connell if he was angry at her the previous night because he went outside while they were dancing, to which Connell responds that he asked her if she wanted to go our for a cigarette, and went on his own when she indicated that she did not. The small-scale echo of their earlier relationship-ending miscommunication emphasises the merits of talking honestly and frankly (something that Marianne is demonstrably able to do). They solve the second, admittedly smaller understanding, because Marianne clarifies the incident with Connell. This suggests that a similarly frank discussion could have saved their relationship earlier on in the novel. They have both grown as people, and are now able to communicate in their relationship more freely.

FURTHER REFLECTION

SOME QUESTIONS TO THINK ABOUT...

- In your opinion, are Connell and Marianne normal people? Why/why not?
- Discuss the growth of Connell and Marianne's characters as the novel progresses.
- Why do you think Marianne dates men, like Jamie and Lukas, who hurt her and make her feel worthless?
- Discuss the place of *Normal People* in the Irish literary canon. What makes it specifically an Irish novel?
- Is *Normal People* a left-wing novel? Why/why not?
- Discuss the presentation of mental health in the novel.
- Discuss the presentation of social status and popularity in the novel.
- Sally Rooney studied English at Trinity College, where she was elected a scholar and participated in the debate team. Given that the same can be said of Connell or Marianne (or both), can *Normal People* be described as autofiction?

We want to hear from you!
Leave a comment on your online library
and share your favourite books on social media!

FURTHER READING

REFERENCE EDITION

- Rooney, S. (2018) *Normal People*. London: Faber & Faber.

BOOK ANALYSIS
Bright Summaries.com
Animal Farm
BY GEORGE ORWELL
The Stranger
BY ALBERT CAMUS
Harry Potter and the Sorcerer's Stone
BY J.K. ROWLING
The Silence of the Sea
BY VERCORS
Antigone
BY JEAN ANOUILH
The Flowers of Evil
BY BAUDELAIRE

www.brightsummaries.com

Ebook EAN: 9782808019057

Paperback EAN: 9782808019064

Legal Deposit: D/2019/12603/119

Cover: © Primento

Digital conception by Primento, the digital partner of publishers.

Printed in Great Britain
by Amazon